The Dreaming Tree

Eithne Massey

Illustrated by Marie Thorhauge
of The Cartoon Saloon

THE O'BRIEN PRESS
DUBLIN

EITHNE MASSEY is the author of *The Secret of Kells* and *Best-Loved Irish Legends* for children.

She has also written two books for adults. She lives between Dublin and Brittany.

First published 2009 by The O'Brien Press Ltd,
12 Terenure Road East, Rathgar, Dublin 6, Ireland.
Tel: +353 1 4923333; Fax: +353 1 4922777
E-mail: books@obrien.ie
Website: www.obrien.ie

ISBN: 978-1-84717-158-0

Kindly supported by

The Department of
Arts, Sport and Tourism
An Roinn
Ealaíon, Spóirt agus Turasóireachta

A catalogue record for this title is available from the British Library

1 2 3 4 5 6 7 8 9 10
09 10 11 12 13 14

Printed and bound in Poland by Białostockie Zakłady Graficzne S.A.
The paper in this book is produced using pulp from managed forests.

Roberto and Amanda were on their way home from school. It was only a short walk through the park. The park was nice. There were lots of trees and flowers. There were lots of children playing. There was a little river.

Roberto had to look after Amanda. She was two years younger than he was. Amanda smiled most of the time. She was not smiling now. She dragged her schoolbag along the ground. She whined.

'You are going too fast,' she said, 'I can't keep up.'

It was true. Roberto was walking as fast as he could. He wanted to get through the park quickly. He did not want to

see the boys playing football. They were always there. They never asked him to come and play.

The biggest boy was called Fergus. Fergus was telling the players what team they were on. Today it was the World Cup. Fergus was the Captain of the Irish team. He was always the Captain. He always got the best players. The goalie, Shane, was his brother. Shane was the same age as Roberto.

Roberto thought he looked nice. He smiled at Roberto
and Amanda as they went past.

When they got home their mother was very excited because their grandmother was going to telephone that afternoon.

'You can both talk to Vovó on the telephone,' she said.

Roberto and Amanda had been born in Rio de Janeiro.
Their grandmother still lived there. Roberto missed her a
lot.

Vovó came on the phone to Roberto. Even though they
often spoke English at home now, Roberto and Amanda

always spoke Portuguese to their grandmother. She didn't speak any English at all.

She said:

'So, you have been in Ireland all summer now. How is your new school? Have you made any friends?'

THE DREAMING TREE

'Not really,' said Roberto.

'But you must,' said Vovó. 'Why go all across the world if you don't make friends? Would you like a friend?'

'Of course I would,' said Roberto.

'Well, I have an idea,' said Vovó. 'You remember the story I told you?'

'Which story?' said Roberto. Vovó had told him many, many stories.

'The one about the Dreaming Tree,' said Vovó.

'Tell me again,' said Roberto.

'There was once a boy who found a tree in the forest. There were all sorts of different animals lying in it. They lay in its branches. They lay around its roots. There were blue and yellow parrots with their heads hidden under

their wings. A snake was curled around a tapir's tail. A squirrel monkey was stretched out on a caiman's back at the bottom of the trunk. There were baby bats hanging from the branches.

'All of the animals were fast asleep. Some of them shifted in their sleep. Some of them made little noises, as if

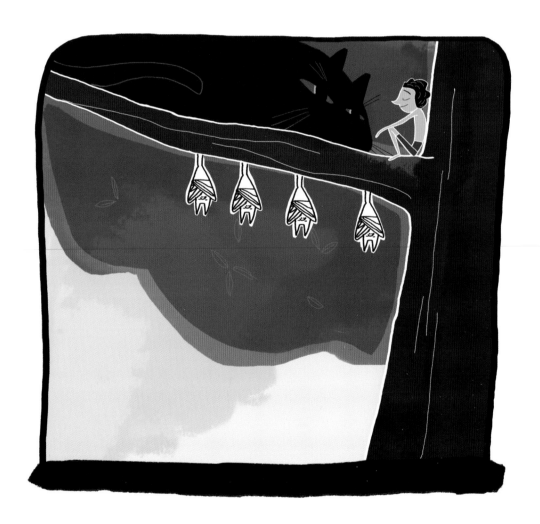

they were dreaming. None of them woke up when the boy climbed into the tree. He fell fast asleep too. He dreamed that he met a big black jaguar. It was the Jaguar King! The Jaguar King taught him many things. When the boy woke and left the tree he had become very wise. He knew how to get his heart's desire.'

'What's a heart's desire?' asked Roberto.

'It is what you really, really want,' said Vovó.

'So, do I have to find a jaguar?' said Roberto. 'I don't think they have them here.'

'No, you have to find a tree,' said Vovó.

Amanda was jumping up and down. She wanted to talk to Vovó.

'Let your sister have a go on the phone,' said his mother. 'This is costing Vovó a fortune.'

Amanda got on the telephone to her grandmother. She told her all about her new friend. Her friend was called Aoife. Tomorrow, Amanda was going to Aoife's birthday party. When she got off the phone she wanted to show Roberto and their mother the new dance she had learned at school.

'You are showing off,' said Roberto.

Amanda didn't care what he said. She kept smiling and dancing.

'She is not showing off,' said his mother. 'Amanda is a good dancer. You are good at football. Why don't you show the boys at school how good you are? It's ok to be proud of what you can do. I am proud that I am such a good gardener!'

Roberto's mother was a very good gardener. Even though there was no garden in the apartment, there was

a balcony. Roberto's mother had filled it with lots of bright flowers. It was the brightest balcony in the block. Roberto's mother loved bright colours. She made Roberto wear blue and red and yellow shirts.

Roberto hated to look different from everyone else. He hid his shirts under a navy sweatshirt. Now he pulled on his sweatshirt. Amanda was still showing off her dance. He asked his mother if he could go out to the park to play.

'Go ahead,' she said. 'But be sure to be back by four o'clock. And come home if it starts to rain.'

'You mean *when* it starts to rain,' said Roberto. Sometimes, he really missed the weather in Rio de Janeiro,

where it was nearly always warm and the sun came out
almost every day.

Roberto went to the park. He thought about what his
mother had said. But he didn't go to where the boys were

still playing football. Instead he thought about his
grandmother's story. He found a big tree.

It was the biggest tree in the park. The tree's branches
stretched far out on every side. Roberto climbed up into

the tree. He could hear the boys playing far away. The sound did not upset him. He felt as if he were a bird in a nest.

The green leaves moved in the sunlight. They went backwards and forwards, backwards and forwards.

The green branches swayed in the wind. Rocking him.
Backwards and forwards, backwards and forwards.

He could hear water flowing and the sound of the
branches moving in the wind and the voices far away.

He fell fast asleep. He dreamed about all the animals his grandmother had told him about.

Roberto opened his eyes. A face was peering at him through the leaves. It was a jaguar! The jaguar was huge and black. Roberto looked into its slanted green eyes.

They were the same colour as the leaves around its black face.

The jaguar opened its mouth in a huge yawn. Roberto could see its white teeth and pink tongue and dark throat. He could hardly breathe. Then he heard a strange noise. The jaguar was purring loudly. It stretched itself.

'I am Sinaa,' it said. 'The Jaguar King. What do you want?'

'I want a friend,' said Roberto. The Jaguar King smiled.

Roberto opened his eyes. Everything was darker. The leaves were a darker green. The sky was a darker blue.

'It must have been a dream,' he thought. 'I must have been asleep.'

But he could still hear purring. He could still see green eyes looking at him through the leaves. He could see white

teeth and a pink tongue. But there was no jaguar there.

Just a very large, fat, black cat. It was curled in the

branches of the tree. It was yawning, as if it had just

woken up. Then it stretched itself.

Roberto could hear voices calling.

'Snowy, come here Snowy, here Snowy ... good cat.' It was Fergus. His voice was high and squeaky. Roberto wondered if he was going to cry.

'Come here, why don't you?' he called again.

Roberto peered down through the branches. Fergus and Shane were beneath the tree, looking very worried.

Shane said, 'Where could she have got to?'

'She'll be all right,' said Fergus.

'She might not be,' said Shane 'She has been missing for ages. She could have her kittens any minute.'

Roberto looked at the cat. The cat looked at Roberto.

'Come here, little cat,' he whispered. The cat came over to him. She let him lift her up.

He scrambled down the tree. It was hard to keep a grip on the cat. But he made it. The two boys jumped when he appeared out of the leaves. Then they saw the cat.

'Is this your cat?' Roberto asked. But he didn't need an answer.

Shane had taken the cat in his arms. He was hugging her tightly. Roberto hoped he wouldn't squeeze the kittens out.

Shane and Fergus were smiling at him. Roberto smiled back.

'Why do you call her Snowy?' he asked. 'She's black.'

'It's a joke,' said Shane. They all started to laugh.

The next day, Roberto walked home through the park by himself. Amanda had gone to Aoife's birthday party. He went past the place where the boys were playing football.

'Hey, come over here,' said Fergus.

Roberto went over.

'Do you want to be on the Irish team?' asked Fergus. 'You will need an Irish granny,' he said. 'What's your granny's name?'

Roberto thought very hard. Then he remembered.

'It's Jacinta Santos Silva,' he said.

'That's ok then,' said Fergus, 'I have an auntie called Jacinta. It's an Irish name. You can play for Ireland.'

Roberto thought for a minute. Ireland had never made it to the World Cup Final. Not once. Brazil had won the World Cup. Five times.

But then he saw Shane grinning at him. Yesterday, Shane had told him that he could have one of Snowy's kittens. Roberto had told Amanda. The kitten was still a secret from their mother. It was going to be a surprise for her.

'I usually play striker,' Roberto said. 'Is that ok?' Fergus nodded his head.

The sun was shining. Roberto pulled off his jacket. His shirt was green and yellow today. It had five gold stars on it.

MARS.

RUSSIA

SIERRA LEONE

NIGERIA

SCOTLAND

CRETE

EGYPT

FRANCE

EIRE

BRAZIL

IRAQ

CZECH REPUBLIC

THAILAND

GREECE

GERMANY.

CANADA.

POLAND

USA
D.